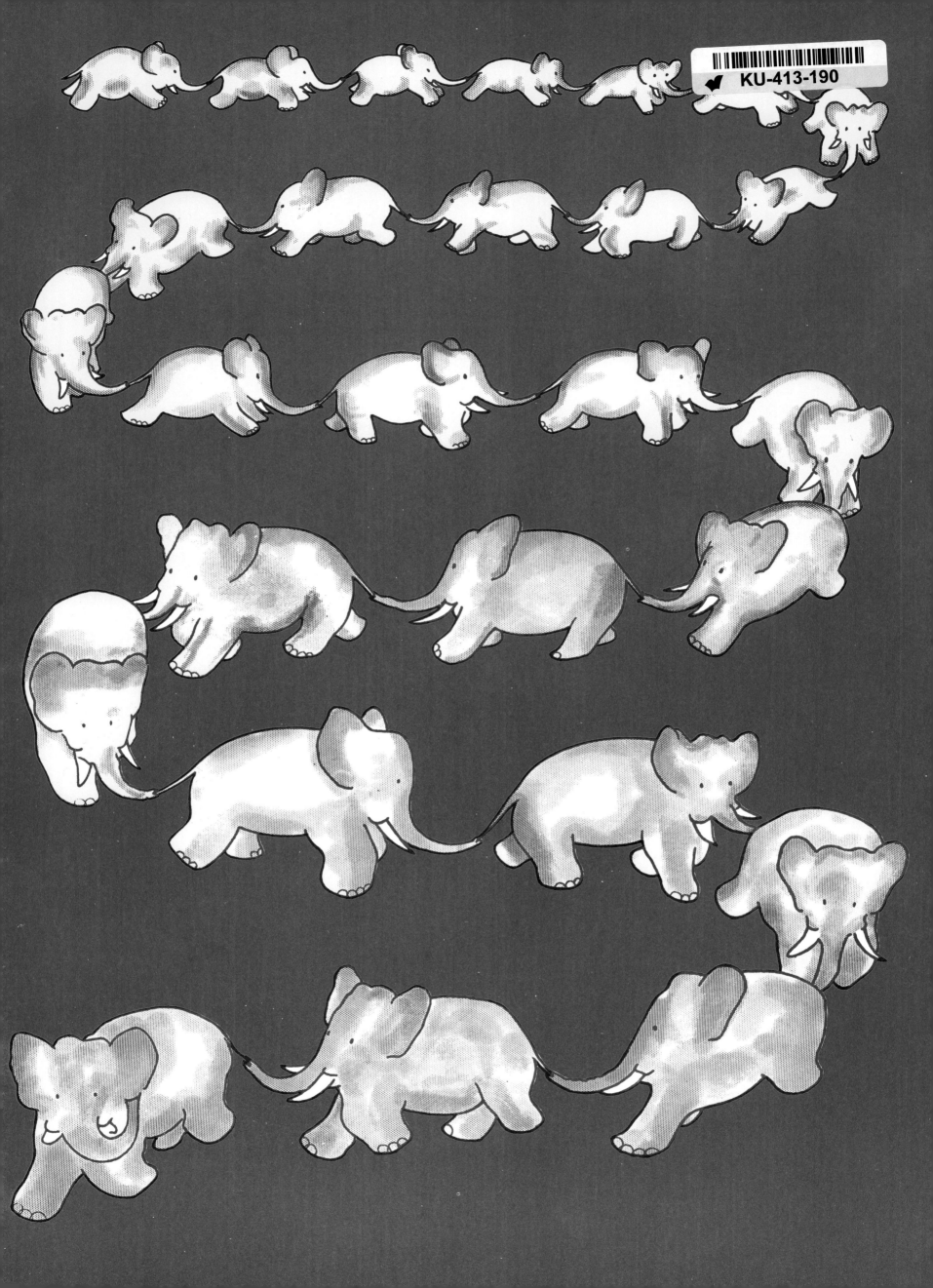

Have you read these other books by
Jean de Brunhoff?

The Story of Babar
Babar the King
Babar's Travels
Babar at Home

JEAN DE BRUNHOFF

BABAR

and
FATHER CHRISTMAS

GRATTIS PÅ
FÖDELSEDAGEN MAX
FRÅN
JAMES

"My friends,"
said the little monkey Zephir one day
to Arthur, Pom, Flora and Alexander,
"listen to the wonderful story
I have just been told.
On Christmas Eve, in the world of Men,
a kind old man
with a long white beard,
in a red coat and a pointed cap,
travels through the air.
He carries many toys with him
which he gives to little children.
He is called Father Christmas.
It is difficult to see him,
for he comes down the chimney while children are asleep.
In the morning they know he has been
because their stockings are full of toys.
Suppose we write to him
and ask him to come to the land of the elephants?"

"Hurrah! What a splendid idea!" said Alexander.
"But what can we put in the letter?" asked Arthur.
"We must tell Father Christmas what we want," suggested Pom.
"Let us think first before we write," added Flora.
They all paused for a moment and thought.

Zephir thought he would like a bicycle,
Flora said she would love a doll,
Alexander wanted a butterfly net,
Pom a big bag of sweets and a baby bear.
As for Arthur, he longed for a railway.

When they had all decided what they wanted,
it was arranged that Zephir,
who had the best handwriting, should write the letter.
So he set about it.
Arthur remembered that one must have a stamp
on the envelope.
Then they all signed the letter,
and went happily to post it.

Every morning the five friends
waited for the postman to come.
As soon as they saw him they ran to meet him.
But, alas!
the postman searched in vain: there was no reply
from Father Christmas.
One day Babar saw them and said to himself:
"What is the matter with the children? They look so sad."

He at once called
them and said:
"Come, children,
what is the matter?"
Zephir told him all about the letter.
"And haven't you had a reply?" asked Babar.
"You must have forgotten to put a stamp on."
No, they said, Arthur had remembered it.
"Then perhaps Father Christmas has not had time
to answer. Don't worry. Go and play.
I believe you have given me a good idea."
Babar got out his pipe and smoked it.
He walked up and down, thinking hard.
"Why didn't I ask Father Christmas
before,
to come to
the land of
the elephants?

It would be a good idea to go at once and look for him. If I talk to him he will not refuse to come." Having made up his mind, Babar at once called Celeste to come and help him pack. Celeste would have liked to go with him, but Babar told her that it would be better if she stayed and ruled the country in his absence, and that mysterious people often did not like to be approached by several people at once. After a good journey Babar arrived in Europe and got out of the train. He had left his crown behind so that no one should recognise him.

He was taken to a quiet little old hotel
and given a nice room,
where he undressed and washed.
One always feels better after a good wash.
"But what is that funny little noise?"
he said as he dried himself.
Without moving he looked carefully round him
and suddenly he saw three baby mice.
The boldest of them said to him:
"Good day, big sir,

Shall we have the pleasure of seeing you here for long?"
"Oh no," replied Babar, "I am only passing through.
I am looking for Father Christmas."
"Looking for Father Christmas!
Why, he is here, in this house!
We know him well," said the little mice.
"We will show you his room."
"Hurrah!" cried Babar in astonishment. "Why, what a
piece of luck! Give me time to put on a dressing-gown
and I will go with you."

"But where are these little mice taking me to?"
he said to himself later,
stopping for a moment on the stairs
to get his breath.
"Father Christmas must have a room
right at the top of the house.
He must be very fond of a good view
and plenty of open space in front of him."
While Babar was thinking this,
the three little mice reached the attic.
But what were they doing so busily
there in the corner?
"Where are you?" called Babar.
"Here, in the attic," replied the little mice.
"Come quickly! We have unhooked Father Christmas!"

When Babar joined them
the little mice said to him happily :
"There is Father Christmas !
He stays quietly here all the year round.
But on Christmas Day they come to fetch him
to put him on the top
of a brand-new Christmas tree.
When the party is over he goes back
to his corner
and we can play with him."
"But this is not the one I am looking for !"
said Babar.
"I want the real Father Christmas,
the living Father Christmas,
not a doll !"

Next morning
Babar heard a tapping at his window.
It was some sparrows, who said to him:
"We hear you are looking for
the real Father Christmas.
We know him very well
and will take you to him."
And they flew gaily away.
They showed Babar the road.
He had to cross the big bridge
over the river.
"We are nearly there," they said.
"He is always somewhere about here.
Usually he sleeps under the bridges."
"Goodness! How funny!" thought Babar.
"There he is! There he is!"
cried the little birds all together.
"He is over there

beside the fisherman."
Babar went down on to the quay
and, a little surprised at the
appearance of the old gentleman,
greeted him and said:
"Excuse me, sir,
but are you really Father Christmas,
who gives toys
to children?"
"Alas, no," replied the old man.
"My name is Lazzaro Campeotti.
I am an artists' model by trade.
My friends the artists
first called me Father Christmas,
and now everyone calls me
by that name."
Babar wandered disconsolately
along the quays, deep in thought.

On the stall of a second-hand bookseller Babar found a big book which contained some pictures of Father Christmas. He promptly bought it, and took it to his room to read. Unfortunately the text was printed in a language he did not know. He explained his difficulty to the manager of the hotel, who kindly gave him the address of a teacher at his son's school. "I am quite sure", he said, "that Mr. Gillianez will be able to translate your book". Without losing any time Babar went to Professor Gillianez's house and rang the bell. The Professor asked him in at once, but after one look at the book declared

he was very sorry
but he could not read it,
and gave him the address of the
celebrated Professor William Jones.
An hour later
Babar found himself
in this gentleman's study.
The Professor examined the book
carefully, uttering little grunts.
At last he said to Babar, who was waiting patiently:
"Your book is very difficult to read.
It is written in old Gothic letters.
It gives details of the life of Father Christmas,
and states that he lives in Bohemia,
not far from the little town of PRJMNESTWE.
But I cannot find any more definite
information on this point."

Babar went and sat down in the park to think things over.
The birds recognised him and came to ask
whether he had yet found Father Christmas.
"Not yet," replied Babar. "All I know is
that he lives a long way from here,
near the town of PRJMNESTWE.
My search is very difficult."
At this moment a little dog who was passing by said to Babar:
"Excuse me, sir, I am very good

at finding lost things, because I have a very sensitive nose.
If only I could smell the doll
belonging to that little girl Virginia over there,
I am sure I could take you to Father Christmas,
for it was he who gave it to her.
I am a stray dog,
and I should be very pleased to go with you."
Babar looked at the little dog and said:
"Very well, I will take you with me."
Then he ran to buy a beautiful new doll
which Virginia gladly changed for hers.
He handed
Father Christmas's
doll to his dog
to smell,
and gave him
a lump
of sugar.

Before leaving, Babar went back to see the wise
Professor William Jones,
who returned the book
and gave him a few useful directions.
It was in a forest, on a mountain,
about fifteen miles from the town,
that Father Christmas must live.
Babar arrived after a difficult journey
at the little town of PRJMNESTWE.

It was cold, and there was a lot of snow,
so Babar made special preparations.
He bought some skis,
and hired a sledge,
and was taken to the foot
of the mountain.
Soon he had to leave the sledge,
and, alone with Duck (that was
the name he had given his dog),
with his skis on his feet
and his knapsack heavily filled,
he climbed towards
the mysterious forest.
Duck was very excited.
He looked round, and yelped softly.
Then he lifted his tail,
stood still, and sniffed.
He must have recognised
the smell
of Father Christmas.

Suddenly
Duck
started
to run.
"I've got it!
I've got it!
The scent!"
he cried,
barking
loudly
and the
whole forest
echoed.
But what was that
moving
in the
wild forest?

It was the little dwarfs of the mountain
hiding behind the tree-trunks!
Duck wanted to go nearer and see them,
but they rushed at him
and bombarded him with hard snowballs,
which
landed
on his head,
in his eyes,
and on
his body.

Half suffocated and half blinded, with his tail between his legs, he ran quickly back to his master. He was out of breath and miserable. Babar stopped when he saw him.

"Good gracious, Duck!" he said. "Whatever has happened?" And Duck told him of his adventure with the little bearded dwarfs.

"Good! We must go up to them!" replied Babar. "I am very curious to make the acquaintance of these gnomes. Take me to them."

Several minutes later
Babar in his turn came face to face
with the little dwarfs.
They tried to frighten him,
and bravely rushed at him
and bombarded him.
But Babar quietly blew on them,
and immediately they fell
on top of each other,
and as soon as they could get up,
disappeared noiselessly.
Babar burst out laughing and went on climbing
behind Duck, who had again found the trail.

The little dwarfs went to find
Father Christmas,
and, speaking all at once, told him
that a big animal
with a long nose
had blown at them so hard
that he had knocked them over,
and had then chased them.
Father Christmas listened with interest.
The little dwarfs added
that when they had run away
the huge animal was quite near,
and that, guided by a nasty little dog,
he was coming straight towards
the mysterious cave of Father Christmas.

It was true that Babar was getting near,
but just then a violent storm burst.
The wind blew so hard that the snow stung
his eyes and skin. He could see nothing.
He struggled on desperately; then, realising
that it was dangerous to insist on going further,
he decided to dig a hole and take shelter.

Next he made a roof with a stick,
his skis and some lumps of snow.
Now they had a little shelter. "How cold it is!"
thought Babar. "My trunk is beginning to freeze!"
Duck also was very tired.
Suddenly Babar felt the earth give way beneath him.
He and Duck disappeared. Where had they fallen?

By mistake they had fallen through a ventilator
into the cave of Father Christmas!
"Father Christmas!" cried Babar. "Duck, we are there!"
Then, overcome with weariness, cold and excitement, he fainted.
"Come, little dwarfs of the mountains, forget your quarrel!
We must undress him and warm him," said Father Christmas.

At once they set to work.
They undressed Babar, and then rubbed him hard
with spirits, using big brushes,
and the dwarf doctor gave him some medicine.
Soon he was drinking good hot soup with Father Christmas,
after thanking him from the bottom of his heart.

While being shown over Father Christmas's house, Babar explained that he had made this long journey especially to ask him to come to his kingdom

N.B. The visit included: the big room where Father Christmas usually lived and where Babar had fallen through the hole that you can see on the right; the toyrooms — for example, the doll room, the soldier room, the fancy-dress room, the train room,

to give toys to the little elephants as he
did to the little human children. Father
Christmas was very touched by this request,

the room of building-toys, the toy animal room, the bat and ball room,
etc. (all these were stored in boxes or sacks); and then the dwarfs'
dormitories, the lifts and the machine-rooms.

but he told Babar that he could not come
to the land of the elephants on Christmas Eve
because he was too tired.
"I had the greatest difficulty last year in arranging
an even distribution of toys to
all the children in the world", he added.
"Oh, Father Christmas," said Babar,
"I do understand, but you know

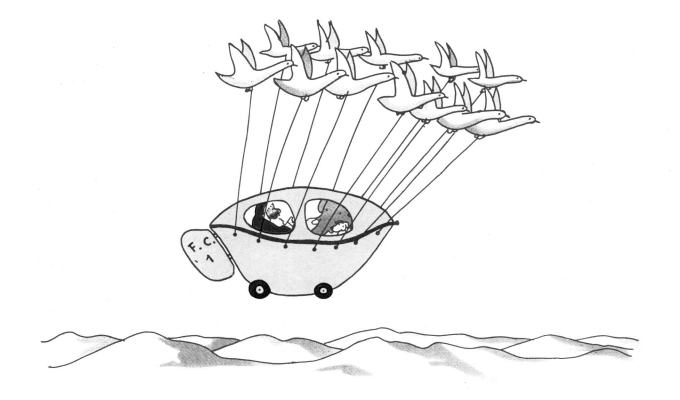

you must look after yourself, get more air, leave
your underground house. "Come with me now
to the land of the elephants and warm yourself in
the sun. You will be rested and better for Christmas."
Pleased by this idea, Father Christmas
commanded the little dwarfs to take care of everything.
Then he went away with Babar and Duck
in his flying machine, F.C. No. 1.

They arrived. Father Christmas admired the scenery.
Elephants came running from all directions
to welcome him.

Pom, Flora and Alexander hurried up. Arthur
clambered on to the roof of a house so that he could
see better, and Zephir climbed a tree. When they were
all quiet at last
Queen Celeste introduced
her three children to
Father Christmas, as well
as Arthur and Zephir.
"Ah! It is you who wrote!"
said Father Christmas.
"I am very pleased to see you,
and I can promise you
a very happy Christmas."

Often
Father Christmas
went out riding
on a zebra.
Babar
went with him
on his bicycle.
But every day
Father Christmas rested for two whole hours in the sun
as Doctor Capoulosse had advised him to.
Sometimes Pom, Flora and Alexander came
to look at him when he was lying in his hammock,
but they were very quiet
so as not to disturb him.

One day
Father Christmas
said to Babar:
"Dear friend,
thank you for all
you have done for me.
Christmas is near, and I must go now and
distribute my toys to the little human children;
they are waiting for them. But I have not forgotten
the promise I made to the little elephants.
Can you guess what I have in this sack?
A real Father Christmas costume
made to fit you! A magic costume
that will enable you to fly through the air,
and a sack that is always full of toys.
You shall take my place on Christmas Eve
in the land of the elephants.
I promise to come back when I have finished my work,
and bring you a beautiful Christmas tree
for your children."

On Christmas Eve Babar did what Father Christmas
had told him. As soon as he had put on the costume and
the beard he felt himself grow light, and began to fly.
"It really is extraordinary," he thought,
"and most useful for distributing toys."

He had to make haste to finish before dawn.
On Christmas morning, in every house, when the
little elephants woke up, what excitement there was!
In the royal palace Queen Celeste
peeped through the door of the room.
Pom was emptying his stocking, Flora nursing her doll;
Alexander jumped up and down on his bed shouting:
"What a lovely Christmas! What a lovely Christmas!"

As he had promised, Father Christmas came back
bringing with him a beautiful tree.
Thanks to him, the family celebration was a great success.

Arthur and Zephir, Pom, Flora and Alexander had never seen anything more beautiful than the firtree sparkling with lights.

The next day
Father Christmas flew away once more
in his machine
back to his underground palace
and his people, the little dwarfs.
On the banks of the big lake
Babar, Celeste, Arthur, Zephir
and the three children
waved their handkerchiefs,
a little sad at seeing their friend
Father Christmas go.
Happily
he has promised to come back each year
to the land of the elephants.

This edition of *Babar and Father Christmas* follows
the first edition in English; it includes the hand-written lettering
which was a feature of the original large format.

This edition first published in Great Britain 10 October 1940
by Methuen & Co. Ltd
Copyright © Librairie Hachette, Paris
Reprinted 2002 by Egmont Books Limited
239 Kensington High Street, London W8 6SA

3 5 7 9 10 8 6 4 2

ISBN 1 4052 0463 X

Printed in France

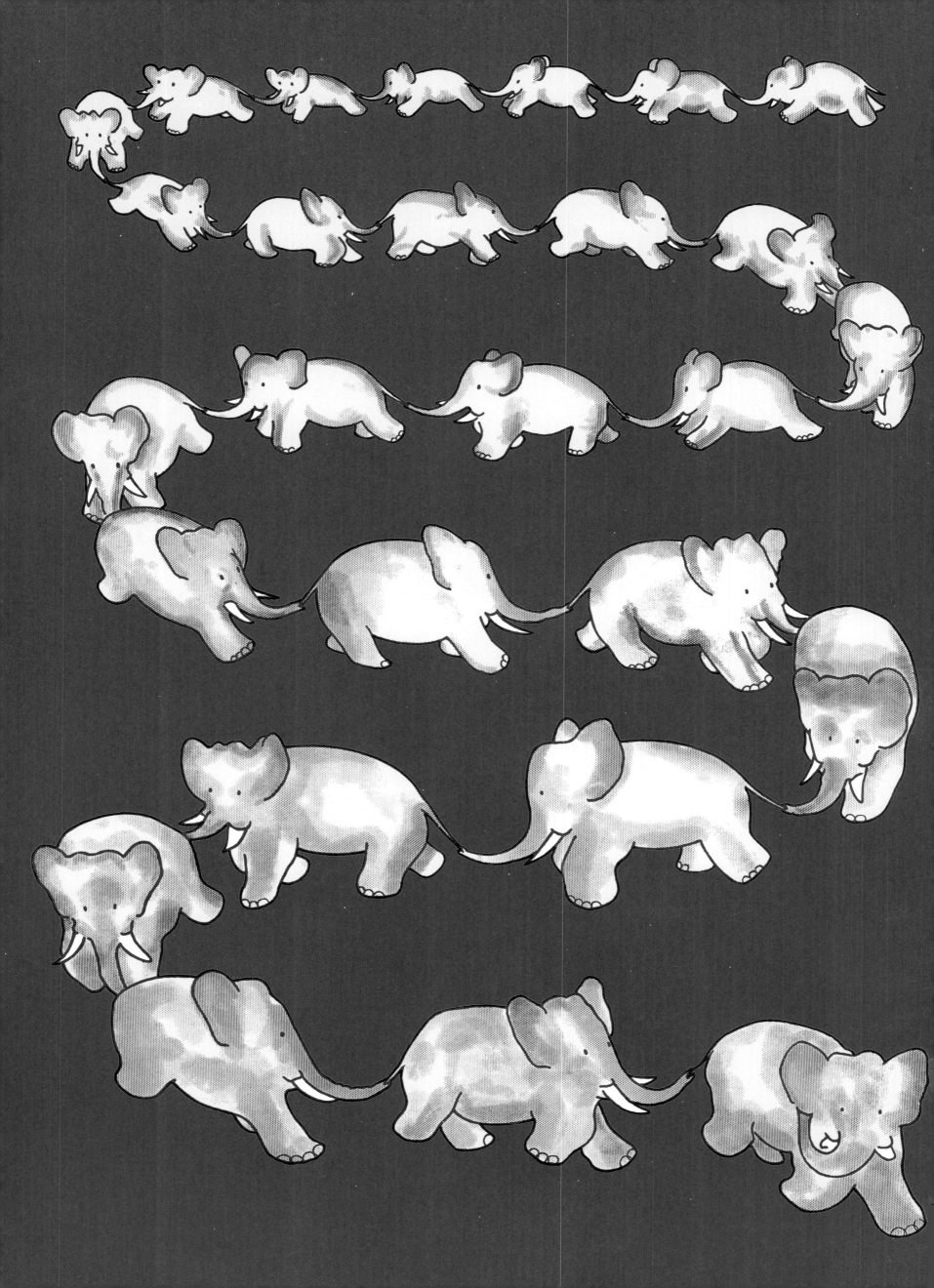